I0797340

EARTH

Becky Noelle

LIGHTBOX
openlightbox.com

Go to
www.openlightbox.com
and enter this book's
unique code.

ACCESS CODE

LBXP4434

Lightbox is an all-inclusive digital solution for the teaching and learning of curriculum topics in an original, groundbreaking way. Lightbox is based on National Curriculum Standards.

OPTIMIZED FOR

- ✓ TABLETS
- ✓ WHITEBOARDS
- ✓ COMPUTERS
- ✓ AND MUCH MORE!

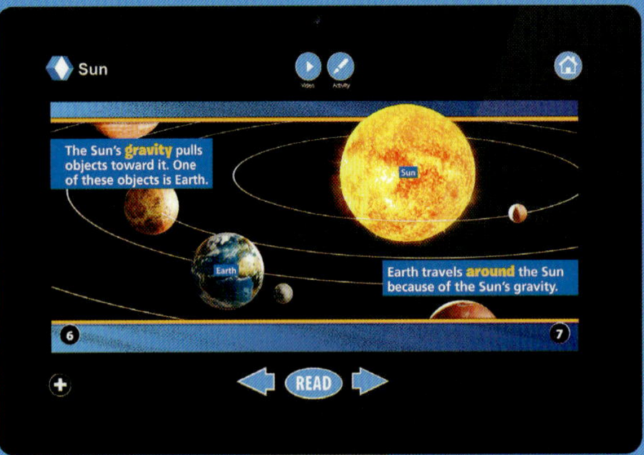

STANDARD FEATURES OF LIGHTBOX

 **AUDIO** High-quality narration using text-to-speech system

 **VIDEOS** Embedded high-definition video clips

 **ACTIVITIES** Printable PDFs that can be emailed and graded

 **WEBLINKS** Curated links to external, child-safe resources

 **SLIDESHOWS** Pictorial overviews of key concepts

 **INTERACTIVE MAPS** Interactive maps and aerial satellite imagery

 **QUIZZES** Ten multiple choice questions that are automatically graded and emailed for teacher assessment

 **KEY WORDS** Matching key concepts to their definitions

VIDEOS

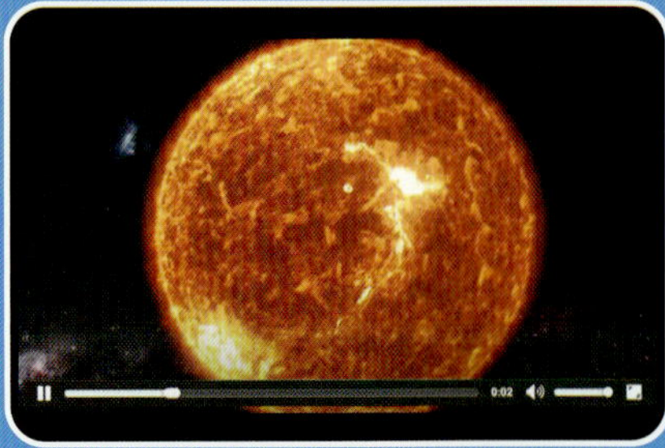

WEBLINKS

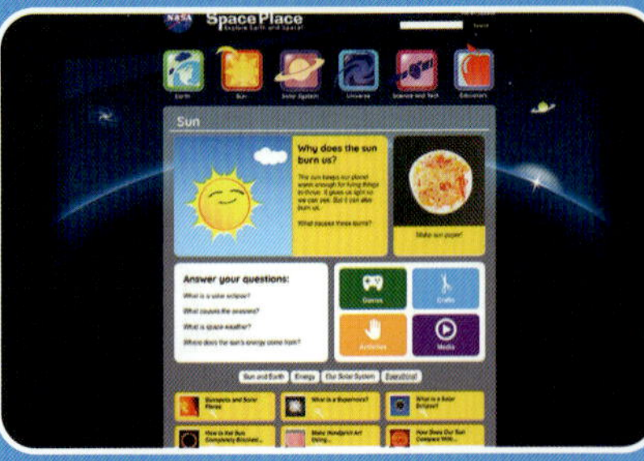

SLIDESHOWS

QUIZZES

EARTH

Contents

Earth is our home. We walk on its surface, breathe its air, and drink its water.

Earth is a **planet** made of rocks and metal. It is the only planet known to have life.

Earth is part of the **solar system**. Earth orbits the Sun with seven other planets.

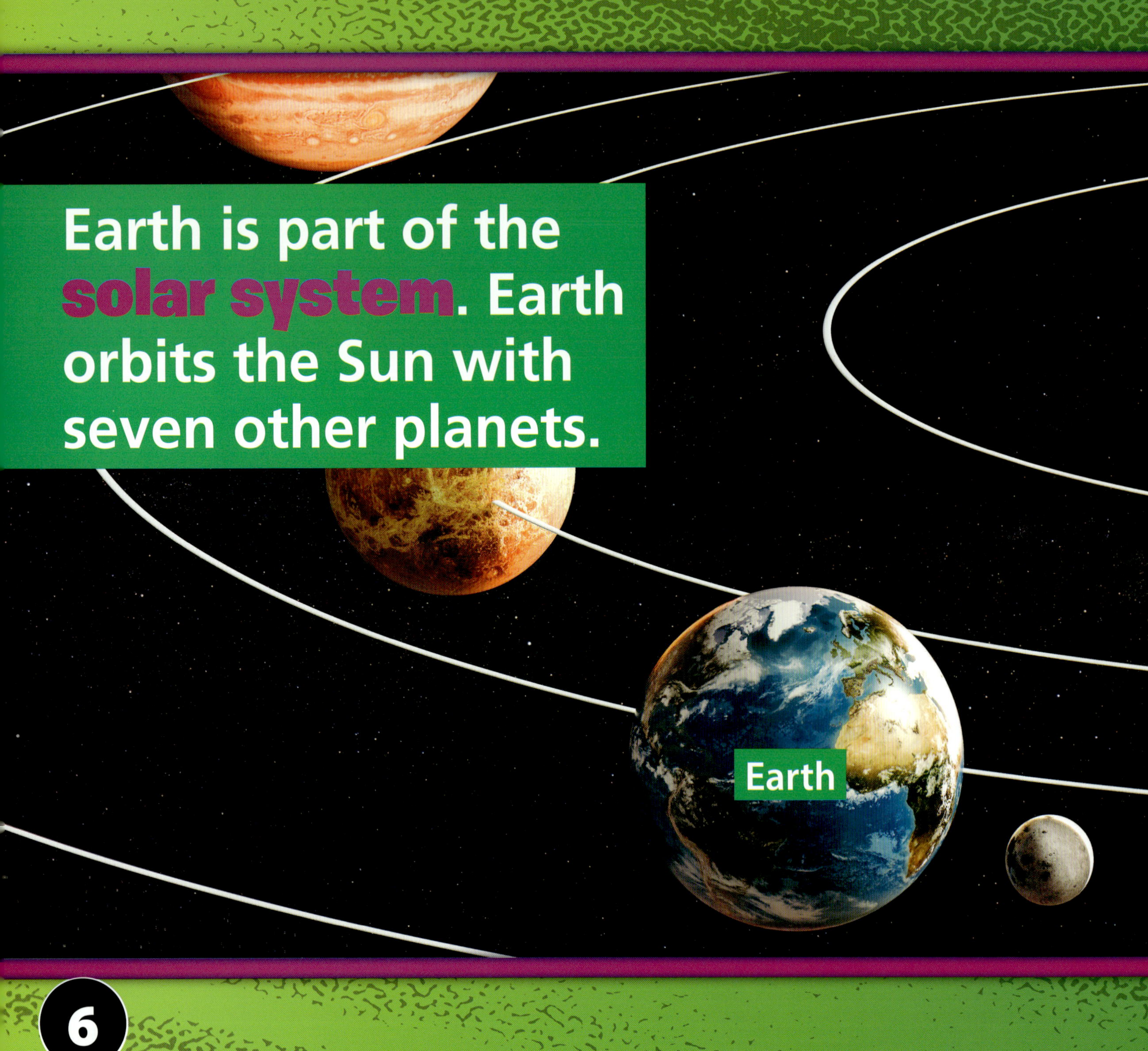

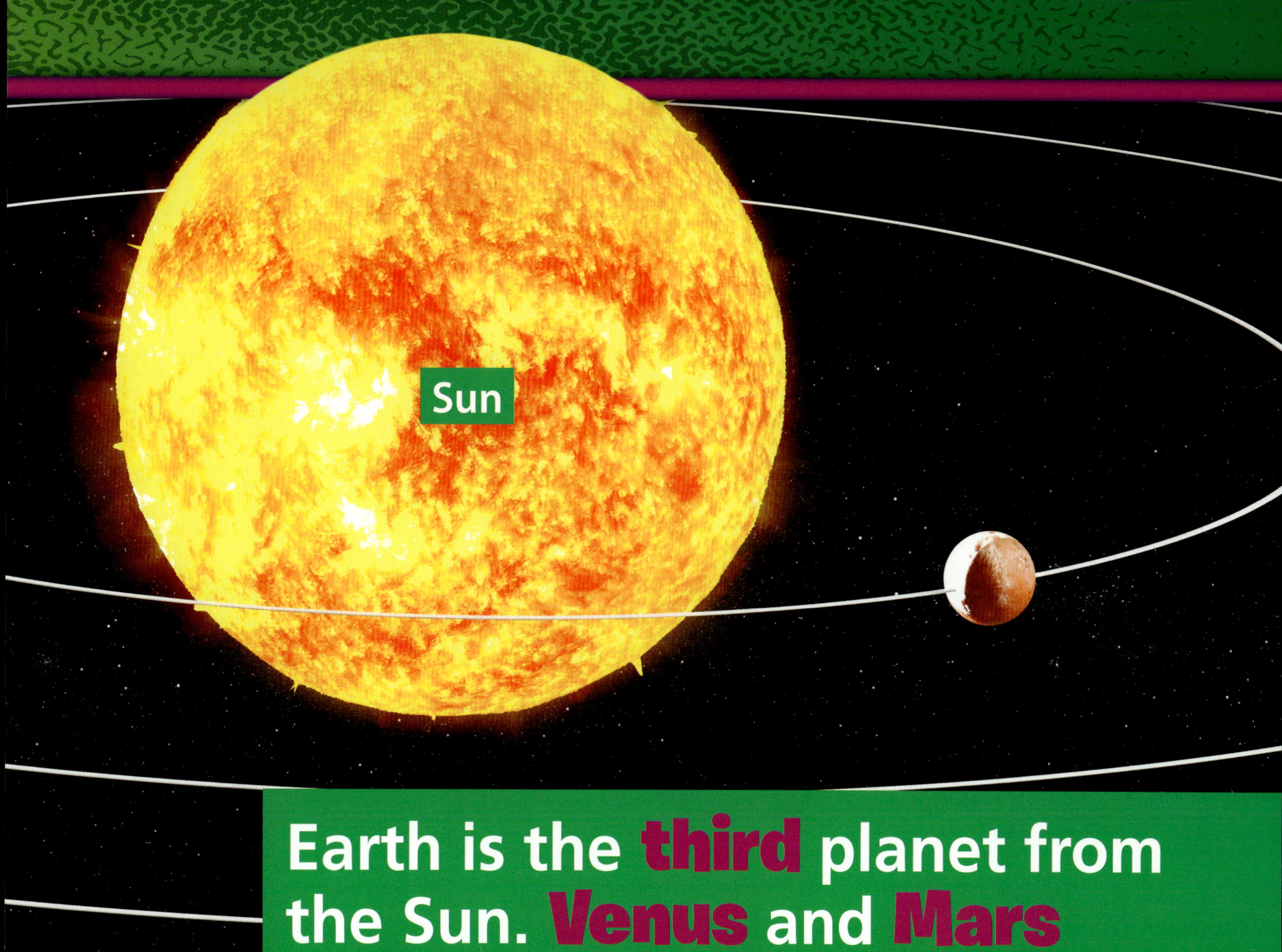

Earth is the **third** planet from the Sun. **Venus** and **Mars** are the planets closest to Earth.

Earth is nicknamed the "**Blue Planet**." From space, Earth looks like a blue marble with white swirls and green parts.

Earth is the **fifth-largest planet** in the solar system.

The blue is **water**. Water covers most of the planet.

Earth is the only planet with the **water** and **air** we need to live.

Earth's **atmosphere** protects us from the Sun's harmful ultraviolet light.

Earth's atmosphere is thinnest at the **North** and **South poles**.

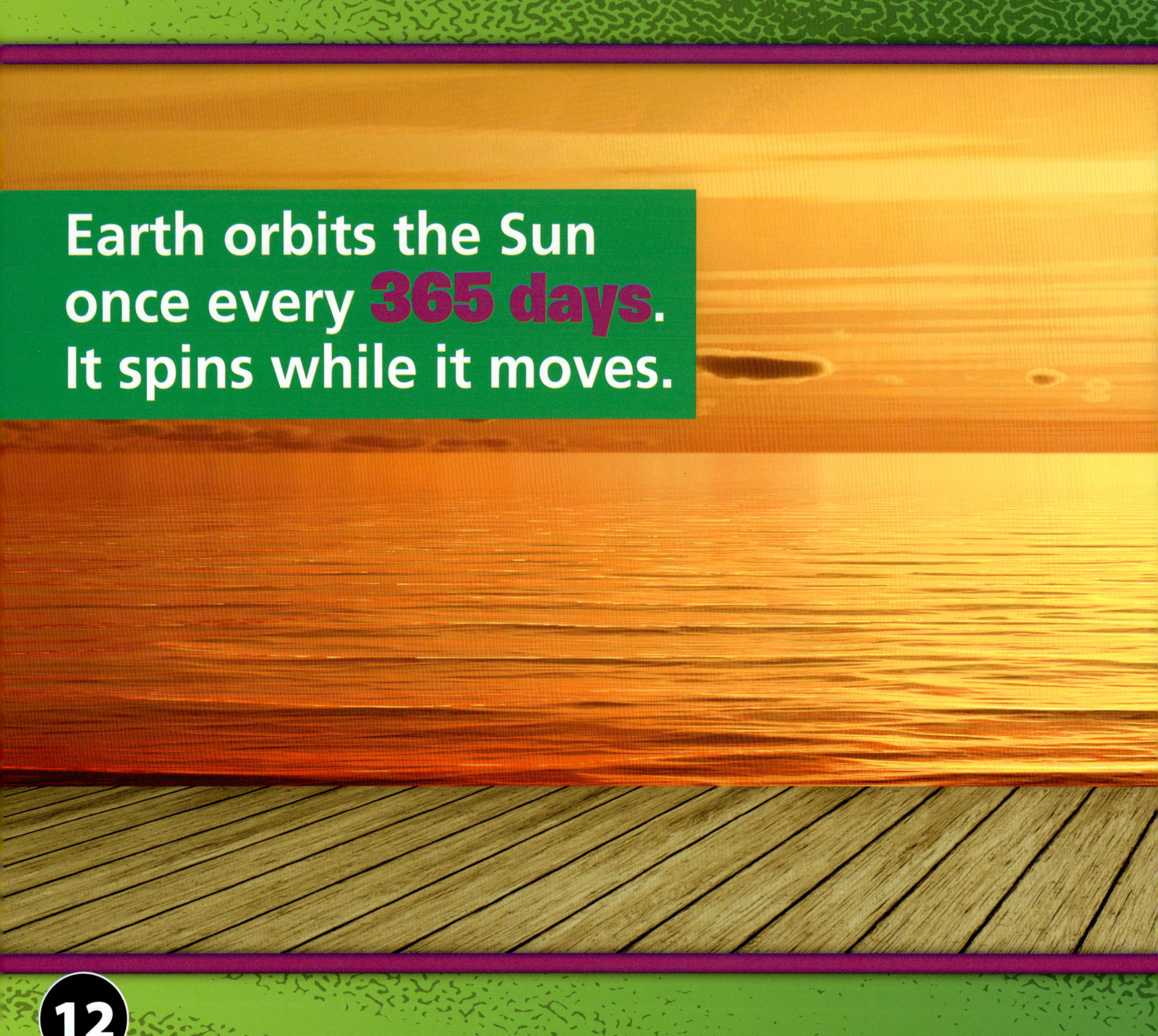

Earth orbits the Sun once every **365 days**. It spins while it moves.

As Earth **spins**, the Sun appears to move through the sky from **east** to **west**.

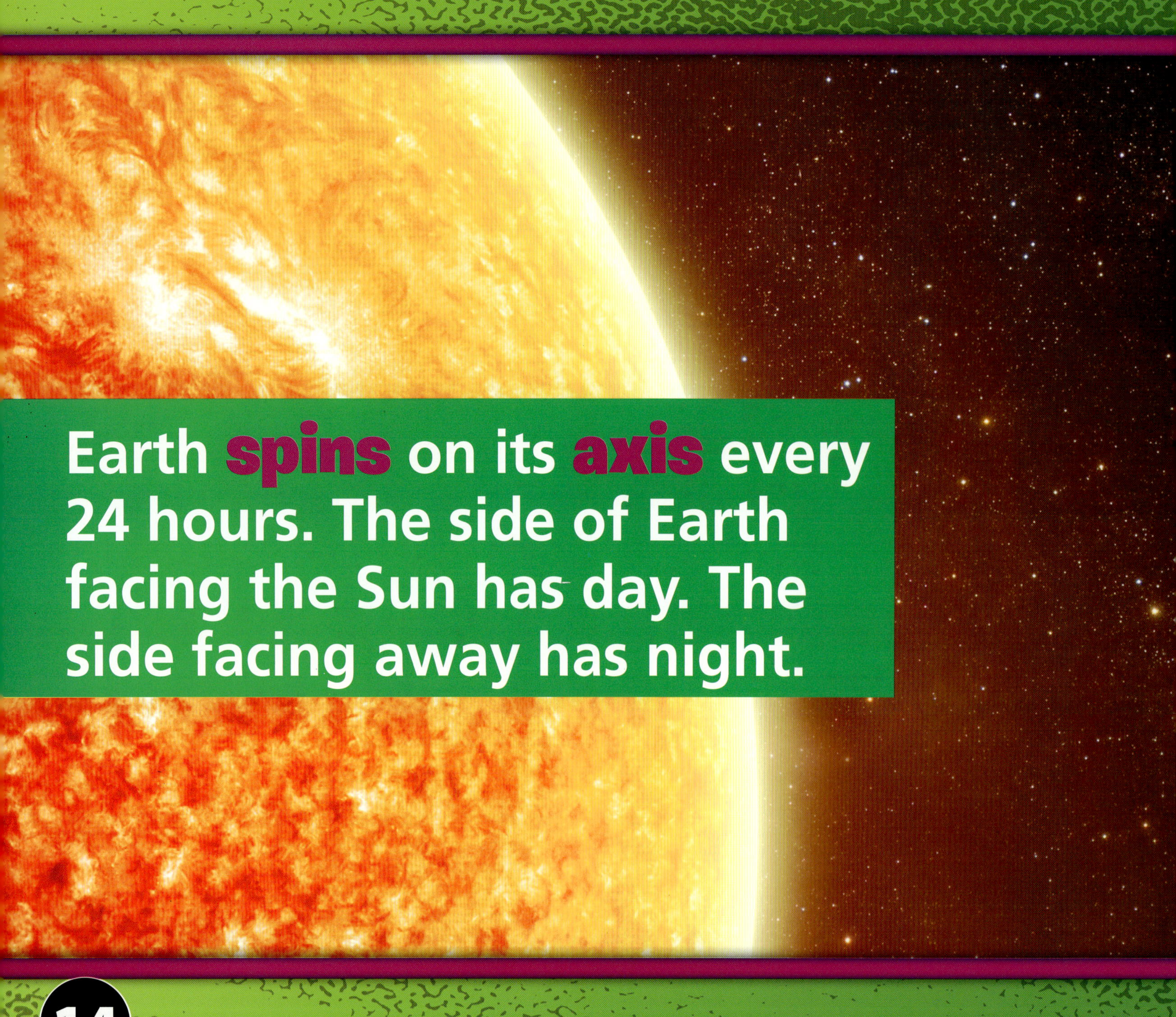

Earth **spins** on its **axis** every 24 hours. The side of Earth facing the Sun has day. The side facing away has night.

Earth is divided into two halves. They are called the **northern** and **southern hemispheres**.

In **summer**, one hemisphere tilts toward the Sun. It is warmed. The other hemisphere tilts away. It has **winter**.

Summer begins in the United States around June. The northern hemisphere **tilts toward** the Sun.

Fall begins in September. The northern hemisphere **starts to tilt away** from the Sun.

Winter begins around December. The northern hemisphere **tilts away** from the Sun.

Spring begins near March. The northern hemisphere **starts to tilt back toward** the Sun.

Scientists study Earth's water, air, and land. They also study Earth from spacecraft orbiting the planet.

Water covers
70 percent of
Earth's surface.

Activity: Season Observations

When does the Sun feel the hottest? How does the Sun's heat affect life on Earth? Find out by observing the Sun and Earth in each season.

Steps

1. Divide a blank piece of paper into four even sections.
2. Label each section with the name of a season.
3. Choose a sunny day in each season to make your observations.
4. Sit in the same spot for each observation.
5. Draw what you see. Include the Sun, clouds, plants, and water.

What did you notice? Does Earth look and feel different in different seasons?

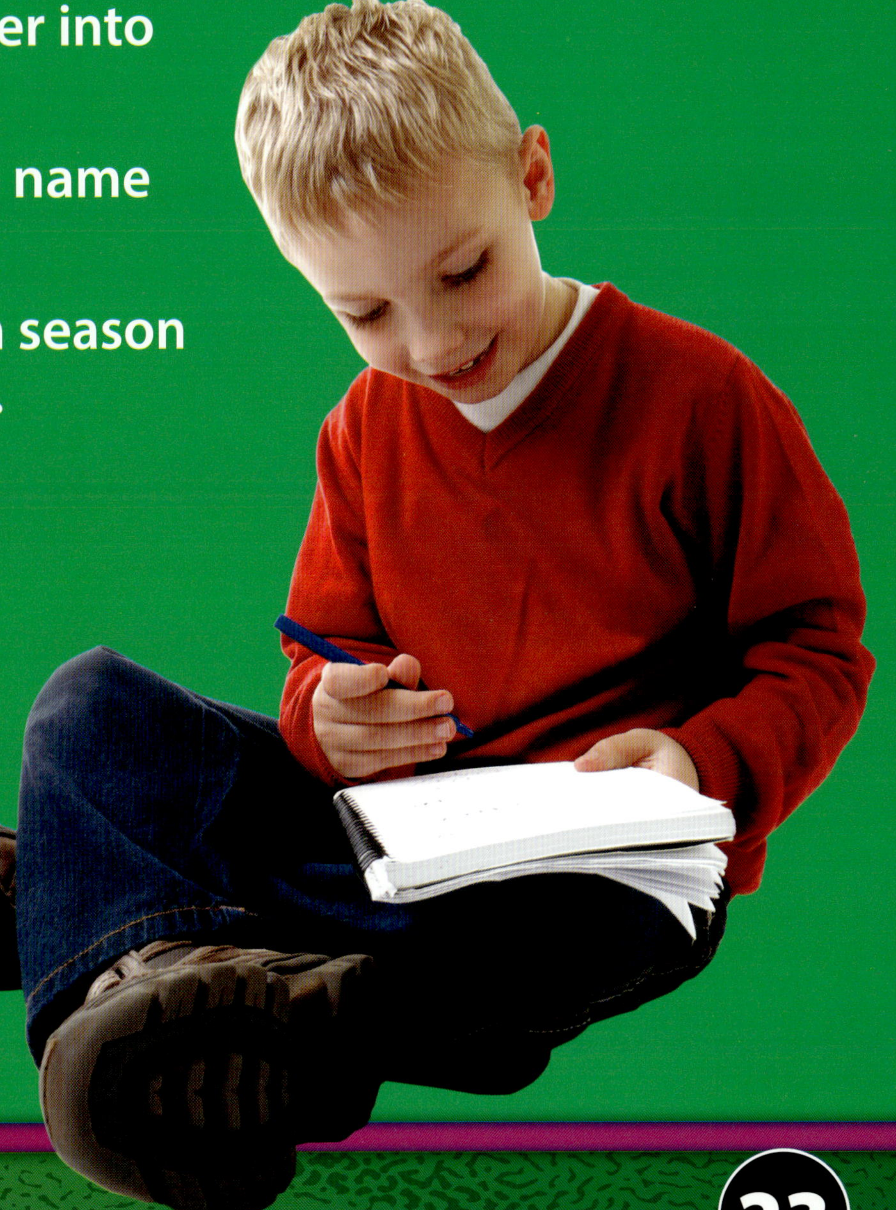

KEY WORDS

Research has shown that as much as 65 percent of all written material published in English is made up of 300 words. These 300 words cannot be taught using pictures or learned by sounding them out. They must be recognized by sight. This book contains 59 common sight words to help young readers improve their reading fluency and comprehension. This book also teaches young readers several important content words, such as proper nouns. These words are paired with pictures to aid in learning and improve understanding.

Page	Sight Words First Appearance
4	a, air, and, Earth, have, home, is, it, its, life, made, of, on, only, our, the, to, walk, water, we
6	other, part, with
7	are, from
8	in, like, looks, white
9	most
10	live, need
11	at, light, us
12	days, every, moves, once, while
13	as, through
14	away, has, night, side
16	into, they, two
17	one
18	around, begins, starts, states
19	back, near
20	also, land, study

Page	Content Words First Appearance
4	metal, planet, rocks, surface
6	solar system, Sun
7	Mars, Venus
8	"Blue Planet," marble, space, swirls
11	atmosphere, North Pole, South Pole
13	east, west
14	axis, hours
16	halves, northern hemisphere, southern hemisphere
17	summer, winter
18	fall, June, September, United States
19	December, March, spring
20	scientists, spacecraft

Published by Smartbook Media Inc.
14 Penn Plaza, 9th Floor New York, NY 10122
Website: www.openlightbox.com

Library of Congress Control Number: 2020936984

ISBN 978-1-5105-5526-6 (hardcover)
ISBN 978-1-5105-5527-3 (multi-user eBook)

Printed in Guangzhou, China
1 2 3 4 5 6 7 8 9 0 24 23 22 21 20

052020
110819

Project Coordinator: Priyanka Das
Designer: Ana María Vidal

Every reasonable effort has been made to trace ownership and to obtain permission to reprint copyright material. The publisher would be pleased to have any errors or omissions brought to its attention so that they may be corrected in subsequent printings.

The publisher acknowledges iStock and Shutterstock as the primary image suppliers for this title.